For Alexander and Rosa
A.MacD.

For K.D. and Mouse
S.F-D.

ISBN 0-590-12026-3

12 11 10 9 8 7 6 5 4 3 2   8 9/9 0 1 2/0

Printed in the U.S.A.

Little Beaver
and
The Echo

Written by Amy MacDonald
Illustrated by Sarah Fox-Davies

A TRUMPET CLUB SPECIAL EDITION

Little Beaver lived all alone by the edge of a big pond. He didn't have any brothers. He didn't have any sisters. Worst of all, he didn't have any friends. One day, sitting by the side of the pond, he began to cry. He cried out loud. Then he cried out louder.

Suddenly, he heard something very strange.

On the other side of the pond, someone else
was crying too.

Little Beaver stopped crying and listened.

The other crying stopped.

Little Beaver was alone again.

"Booo hooo," he said.

"Booo hooo," said the voice from across the pond.

"Huh-huh-waaah!" said Little Beaver.

"Huh-huh-waaah!" said the voice
from across the pond.

Little Beaver stopped crying. "Hello!" he called.

"Hello!" said the voice from across the pond.

"Why are you crying?" asked Little Beaver.

"Why are you crying?" asked the voice from across the pond.

Little Beaver thought for a moment. "I'm lonely," he said. "I need a friend."

"I'm lonely," said the voice from across the pond. "I need a friend."

Little Beaver couldn't believe it. On the other side of the pond lived somebody else who was sad and needed a friend.

He got right into his boat and set off to find him.

It was a big pond. He paddled and paddled.

Then he saw a young duck, swimming in circles

all by himself.

"I'm looking for someone who needs a friend,"

said Little Beaver. "Was it *you* who was crying?"

"I do need a friend," said the duck. "But it

wasn't me who was crying."

"I'll be your friend," said Little Beaver.

"Come with me."

So the duck jumped into the boat.

They paddled and paddled. Then they saw a
young otter, sliding up and down the bank
all by himself.

"We're looking for someone who needs a friend,"
said Little Beaver. "Was it *you* who was crying?"

"I do need a friend," said the otter. "But it
wasn't me who was crying."

"We'll be your friends," said Little Beaver and
the duck. "Come with us."

So the otter jumped into the boat.

They paddled and paddled. Then they saw a young turtle, sunning himself all alone on a rock. "We're looking for someone who needs a friend," said Little Beaver. "Was it *you* who was crying?"

"I do need a friend," said the turtle. "But it wasn't me who was crying."

"We'll be your friends," said Little Beaver and the duck and the otter. "Come with us."

So the turtle jumped into the boat, and they paddled and paddled until they came to the end of the pond. Here lived a wise old beaver, in a mud house, all alone. Little Beaver told him how they had paddled all around the pond, to find out who was crying.

"It wasn't the duck," he said. "It wasn't the otter. And it wasn't the turtle. Who was it?"

"It was the Echo," said the wise old beaver.

"Where does he live?" asked Little Beaver.

"On the other side of the pond," said the wise old beaver. "No matter where you are, the Echo is always across the pond from you."

"Why is he crying?" said Little Beaver.

"When you are sad, the Echo is sad," said the wise old beaver. "When you are happy, the Echo is happy too."

"But how can I find him and be his friend?"
asked Little Beaver. "He doesn't have
any friends, and neither do I."

"Except for me," said the duck.

"And me," said the otter.

"And me," said the turtle.

Little Beaver looked surprised. "Yes," he said,
"I have lots of friends now!"
And he was so happy that he said it again,
very loudly: "I have lots of friends now!"
From across the pond, a voice
answered him: "I have
lots of friends now!"

"You see?" said the wise old beaver. "When you're happy, the Echo is happy. When you have friends, he has friends too."

"Hooray!" shouted Little Beaver and the duck and the otter and the turtle, all together.

And the Echo shouted back to them: "Hooray!"

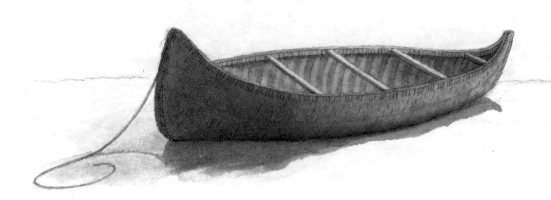